FIC
FIF

J   Fife, Dale.
     The fish in the castle.

THE FISH IN THE CASTLE

The Andersons' vacation was nearly over. Everyone but Eric had a treasure to take home. More than anything else he wanted to catch a grunion. Every evening the family went to the shore to see if the grunion were running. But they were beginning to doubt that the small silver fish even existed — except Eric.

Then Eric found an unexpected ally in Mr. Musante, the fisherman who generally avoided tourists. And that night in an exciting midnight adventure at the beach, Eric surprised the whole family.

Dale Fife captures a various magic and beauty of sea and sky along the California coast in this delightful story of a boy's perseverance and determination — and the unforgettable moment which is his reward.

The FISH
in the CASTLE

by
DALE FIFE

Illustrated by Marilyn Miller

Coward-McCann, Inc.   New York

Library of Congress Catalog Card Number: 65-20378

MANUFACTURED IN THE UNITED STATES OF AMERICA

To Helen and Oliver

ERIC was sure that this was the very best part of the vacation day — sundown, suppertime, with Dad, Mom, Steven, Karen and himself around the beach bonfire, toasting hot dogs.

From where he sat facing the ocean, his back to the Palisade, a dark cliff rising steeply to the sky, he could count six fires along the half-moon curve of the beach. They belonged to trailer-tourists who, like the Andersons, were camped at Pacific Cove. Later, the children, and most of the grown-ups, would go "grunion hunting." No one had seen this fish, much less caught one, but hunting it was great fun just the same.

"Say, my hot dog's on fire," Steven cried, holding up the smoking wiener.

Lazily, Dad passed Steven the box of buns. Dad on vacation was different from Dad at home. Here he didn't rush about anything. He read and flopped and dozed. Now he stretched his long arms and yawned. "This rest was just what I needed."

Mom poured lemonade from the jug. "I got a good tan," she said. Her face in the firelight didn't look tanned. It was rosy as her sweater and head scarf.

Steven slathered his hot dog with mustard. "Wait until the fellows back home see the picture Dad took of the twenty-five-pound tuna I caught. I'm going to frame it and hang it over my bed."

" No one else found a devil shell like mine," Karen said, tossing her long bob. "It's my best souvenir."

Each day Karen had said she was going to the library to find out what kind of shell it was, but so far she had not found the time. The shell was black and rough and big as a football. She planned to use it as a doorstop in her room at home.

Eric didn't have anything special to take home. Not yet. He had tried to find something. He wasn't old enough to go deep-sea fishing like Steven, and Mom wouldn't let him wander beyond the Cove as Karen did with her friend Kathy, whose family was camped right next to them atop the Palisade. Dad had rented a trailer for two weeks. Living in the midget house was fun, especially the sleeping. Steven, who was twelve, and Karen, who was ten,

slept in bunks which made up into couches during the day. Eric, being the youngest, got to sleep on the floor between them in a sleeping bag. Each morning, before anyone stirred, he crept out of his cocoon to sit outside on the trailer step and watch another day begin.

No two days started exactly alike, although some things were the same, like the waves riding in high and mighty, then crash-landing, and tumbling along the sand like spilled soapsuds. Sometimes a lone sea gull wandered along the shore, then again the air sang with flashing wings. Over all were the smells — kelp, fish, salt air. When cottony fog hugged the sea and crept over the brown hills, the day began with mystery and promise — and Eric would be certain he'd find his treasure. Something to put on his special shelf at home; something to remember this vacation forever; something truly his own.

So far he'd had no luck.

Now, sitting around the fire, he saw the first star of the evening shine out of the blue-black sky. "I wish, I wish to find a treasure," he said aloud.

"Well, you'd better hurry," Karen said. "We're leaving day after tomorrow."

Three boys ran past the bonfire. They had their jeans rolled high and were carrying buckets and shovels. "The grunion are sure to run tonight," they shouted. "It's high tide."

"Good luck," Steven shouted.

"They'll need it," Karen said, but just the same she began rolling up her jeans.

Eric had heard many stories about the grunion: that it came right out of the ocean and danced on the sand; that it *always* came in bright moonlight; that it *never* came on moonlight nights; that it was really all one big joke played on the tourists by the native Californians.

"It's just a waste of time, hunting for the ghost fish," Steven said.

"It could be real," Eric said.

Both Steven and Karen hooted.

"If we knew a native Californian, we could ask about it," Mom said.

"There's Mr. Musante," Eric said.

"You mean Old Moustache Cup," Steven said. "I'll bet he's laughing in his beard at us for running around 'hunting' a fish."

Moustache Cup ran a fish shack. It was perched atop the pier. He acted as if he owned the beach, and people said he had lived here forever. Eric knew he would never have the nerve to ask Old Moustache anything. Just looking at his shack made Eric shiver. An eery light shone through its

11

window. Moustache was probably out chasing kids right now. He hated campers and picnickers on the beach.

"I'm ready," Karen said, jumping to her feet.

Steven reached for the bucket and shovel.

But Eric was ahead of them, sprinting to the water's edge.

He crouched low on the sand, rolling up his jeans, searching the tumbling breakers.

Eric knew that some of the campers half-believed there was a fish called grunion. But most of them didn't believe at all. He didn't want to admit it to Karen and Steven, but when he was close to the swirling water, as he was now, with the deep-throated song of the sea in his ears, and the salt spray on his face, he too half believed.

What would a grunion be like? He thought maybe it was as small as a sea horse; as bright as a winking star; as quick as a water bug.

Where did it live?

In a water meadow? An ocean forest? A coral castle?

A CORAL CASTLE, Eric decided. He imagined it swimming in and out of the castle's rosy doors. He could catch it when it did its dance in the moonlight.

Suddenly, Eric saw bits of silver glimmering on the sand.

"Grunion!" he shouted. *"Grunion!"*

Children from other bonfires took up the cry: *"Grunion! The Grunion are running!"*

Karen and Steven came racing.

Eric threw himself headlong onto the wet sand, his fingers grasping the silver. He opened his fist. It was filled with sand.

"I thought I had one," he said to the circle of children.

"Moonbeams," Karen said. "That's what you had."

Eric felt foolish. It wasn't the first time he had mistaken the moon's reflection on the wet sand for grunion.

"Don't take it so hard, fellah," Steven said. "It's just a fake fish."

Steven and Karen were already toasting marshmallows when Eric got back to the fire. Dad moved over and made a place on his blanket for him. Mom handed him the box of marshmallows and Eric stuck one on his pointed stick. He did it carefully, and he held it just close enough to the coals to toast evenly.

Steven burned his. He made funny faces as he nibbled its black edges. This gave Karen the giggles.

14

"The only one in this family who can toast a marshmallow properly is Eric," Mom said. "See, his is golden and crusty on the outside, which means soft and creamy on the inside."

"He thinks about what he's doing," Dad said.

Steven struck a comic pose. "Ah yes, the great marshmallow thinker."

This made Karen go into titters, and Eric threw a handful of sand at Steven. Eric didn't want to be just a good marshmallow toaster. He wanted to be a famous treasure finder.

Mom closed the picnic basket. "Well, it's about that time . . ."

But Eric didn't want to leave. He thought he'd like to stay here forever. Maybe he'd be a beach-comber. When he refused to budge, Karen and Steven jerked the blanket out from under him, dumping him onto the sand.

He picked himself up and raced to the water. The beach was empty — waiting. Far, far away, the stars were blinking secrets. The moon shining on the dark water made a path of silver that stretched to his feet. Suddenly it was all very clear to Eric — a wonderful treasure was near. All he needed to do was reach out and grasp it.

"Eric." It was Dad calling.

15

When he got back, Steven was sand-smothering the coals. "What do you say we do something different tomorrow night, Dad? It's our last," he said.

"I'm with you," Karen said.

"But I haven't found my treasure yet," Eric cried.

"You've had two weeks. What are you looking for?" Steven asked.

"How do I know until I find it," Eric said.

"Just pick up a few shells," Karen said.

"No, I want something special . . . like a grunion."

"Forget about that ghost," Karen said.

Dad gave Eric a playful swat. "You find out for sure there really is such a fish, and we'll have a last bonfire tomorrow night."

"How is he going to do that?" Karen asked, leading the way up the steep steps to the top of the Palisade.

How?

Eric was still wondering next morning as he ate breakfast with Karen and Steven in the trailer. Dad had left early to have the car serviced, ready to take off for home tomorrow.

Steven and Karen were arguing.

"It's your turn to take the books back to the library," Steven said.

"I can't," she said. "Kathy and I are going to hunt kelp along the shore and make hula skirts."

"I'm meeting Jim and some of the fellows for beach ball," Steven said.

"Someone has to take them back," Mom said, coming into the kitchen from the bedroom end of the trailer. "The librarian was kind to let us have a temporary card."

"Eric hasn't anything to do," Karen said.

But he did. He had to find out about the grunion. Still, he was the family errand runner, and it was one of the few things he was allowed to do all by himself. "Okay," he said.

The library, brown as driftwood, was perched atop the Palisade at the opposite end from the pier and Moustache's shack. There were two ways to reach it: by sidewalk from the top of the Palisade, or by walking along the beach. Eric decided to walk along the beach. The morning fog hid the water, all but its lacy edge. The sand felt gritty between his toes until a wave found them and tickled them clean.

He stopped to inspect a sand dollar and six shells which the tide had brought in and set down

18

in a pattern to match the curve of the beach and the Palisade. He didn't collect rocks and shells as Karen did because he didn't think they looked as pretty standing on the trailer patio as they did on the beach awash with salt water, the colors gay as a rainbow. But he did pick up the sand dollar to wish upon. He closed his eyes: "I wish, I wish — to prove there really is a grunion."

A family of "the least sandpipers" came skimming along the shore. Eric stood still and watched the birds chase the rollers back to sea, gobbling up the hoppers washed out by the waves. He supposed they were called "the least" because they were the smallest. Was he then "the least Anderson?"

The sandpeeps chatted with each other: "Cherk–cherk–cherk."

"Don't call me a jerk," Eric said.

At once the flock took off like a single bird, twinkling high over the sea.

And Eric took off for the library.

Eric wandered through the aisles of books. He knew, because Dad had told him, that everything of importance was written down somewhere. Then someone must have written about a grunion. He decided to ask Miss Jennifer, the librarian.

"Well, I've never really seen one," she said. "But let's see what the dictionary says."

Eric watched her finger walk down the page of the dictionary and stop. "Yes, here it is." She read aloud:

"A silversides of the California Coast. Color gray-green above, silver below, bluish line down each side; length four to six inches. Genus *Leuresthes tenuis.*"

20

Miss Jennifer closed the book. "Yes, I would say there is a grunion."

Eric could hardly wait to tell the family. He raced out of the library, down the steps and along the shore. He saw Steven and a group of boys tossing a ball and he ran to them. "Steven, Steven, grunion is in the dictionary," he cried.

Steven gave him a playful jab to the shoulder. "That's the *only* place it is, fellah."

Eric's enthusiasm collapsed.

Then he spied Karen and Kathy along the shore, trailing yards of kelp behind them. He ran to catch up. "Grunion is in the dictionary," he shouted.

Karen grinned. "So is dinosaur, but no one has seen one in millions of years."

Eric trudged on home, hands in the pockets of his jeans.

Just as he reached the trailer, the sun dazzled through the fog. Far out on the blue silk sea Eric saw a red-colored freighter. Maybe it was bound for China. A boy named Greg, with whom Eric sometimes played on the beach, had told him that if you dug deeply enough in the sand you would reach China. He knew this was just make-believe. But maybe if he dug a deep, deep hole, he could trap a grunion. Since he didn't know what else to do he'd try it. He'd get the shovel.

Inside the trailer, Mom was just taking a pan of sugar cookies from the oven. Eric reached for one, but Mom shook her head. "Too hot," she said. She started talking more to herself than to Eric. "I wish Dad were back so I could drive over to the pier and get some sand dabs for dinner. Sometimes the fish shack is closed afternoons."

Eric didn't offer to go. He didn't want to get close to Mr. Musante — Old Moustache Cup. The children on the beach told such scary stories about him. Eric watched Moustache every day, but always from a safe distance.

Late afternoons, when the beach was almost empty, Old Moustache took a run along the shore. With his pants rolled above his bony knees, his arms crooked against his sides, he never stopped until he reached the flat-topped rock which stood almost exactly in the center of the half-moon of the beach. There he rested, huffing and puffing, before racing back. It was hard to tell what he looked like, for his bushy eyebrows and bristly beard made his face into a scrub brush.

Mom was still fussing about the sand dabs. Eric thought he was safe enough; she wouldn't ask him to do two long errands the same morning.

But supposing he did go!

Would he have the nerve to ask Moustache

about the grunion? No, he didn't think he would. But still, how could he know unless he tested himself?

"I'll go," he said recklessly.

Mom was mighty quick to take him up on the offer. Already she was handing him the coin purse from her apron pocket. "Tell Mr. Musante, enough for a family of five."

Now he was into it.

Mom handed him a waxed bag with two sugar cookies in it. "Better get started," she said. It was clear that she had no idea of the danger into which she was sending him.

Eric stuck the bag in his hip pocket along with the coin purse and went outside and down to the beach. As he started walking toward the pier, the sun shining on Moustache's shack made it seem on fire. The closer Eric got to it, the more slowly he moved.

He ambled in the tracks of a seagull, crossing and crisscrossing the sand.

He saw a Portuguese man-of-war washed up on the shore. It looked like a mold of purple jelly, and even though it was the only thing on the beach that was not running or flying, it seemed alive. He knew it was not, but its colors were. Eric crouched low

to the sand and thought about this for quite a while.

A crane flew overhead, whooping that it was heading someplace in a hurry, and this reminded Eric that he too was supposed to be in a hurry.

At the steps which led up to the fish shack he hesitated. The slap-slap of water against the pier's pilings warned: *"Be-ware! Be-ware!"* The warning followed him right up the steps.

Five seagulls, like a row of dozing grandfathers, sat on the railing alongside the shack. They didn't budge at his approach. Well, *they* weren't afraid. Eric squared his shoulders and, whistling, pushed through the screen door.

Old Moustache stood behind the counter cleaning fish. Knife in hand, he turned around. His sweat shirt had a skull and crossbones across the front of it. His face was all wrinkles and bristles.

"WELL! What is it?" he boomed. He looked so fierce, Eric wanted to turn and run, but his legs felt as if they were knee-deep in sand. He couldn't move. He swallowed twice, but no words came.

"Out with it," Moustache shouted. "I haven't got all day."

"My mom wants some sand dabs," Eric managed to squeak.

"Sand dabs? Are you sure?"

"No . . . yes . . ." Eric stammered, wanting to back away. Instead, he stiffened, looked Moustache right in the eye, and spoke up. "Enough for five people."

"You from the village?" Moustache asked.

"We're in a trailer," Eric said. Then, remembering how Moustache felt about campers, he quickly added, "We're leaving tomorrow."

"First time a camper had sense to order sand dabs," Moustache said. "Best eating fish there is. Lots of bones, but worth every last one. You must have a smart mom."

Eric was surprised and pleased at the way the conversation was going. When he reached into his pocket for the coin purse, the sack of cookies came with it. He opened it, and held it out to Moustache. "My mom made them," he said.

Moustache took one and bit into it. "Dee — LISH — ous! I haven't tasted a cookie like this in years."

His eyes, beneath the bushy brows, twinkled. It made them seem as blue as Karen's. Why Moustache was nice. He was very old, probably the very oldest person on the beach. If anyone had ever seen a grunion, it would be Moustache. Suddenly, Eric was not one bit afraid to ask. "Have you ever seen a grunion?"

29

"Thousands of them," Moustache said, and Eric looked to see if he were laughing. He wasn't.

"We didn't see any last night," Eric said. "It was hightide."

"If I were a grunion, you wouldn't have caught me coming in last night." He leaned over the counter. "Can you keep a secret from everyone but your family?"

"Promise."

"All right then. The grunion will hit the beach tonight exactly ten minutes after midnight."

"*Thank you*," Eric cried, grabbing his package and running out of the shack.

He ran most of the way home, and rushed to the patio alongside the trailer where everyone was gathered and Dad was barbecuing hamburgers for lunch. "Moustache — Mr. Musante told me the grunion will run at ten minutes after midnight," he announced breathlessly.

Karen looked up from stringing shells and giggled. "I suppose they tell time by their waterproof wristwatches."

"Not wristwatches," Steven said, between bites of raw carrot. "The head grunion wears an alarm clock around his neck. A million grunion gather in the ocean. The head shouts into his megaphone: 'Now hear this! Now hear this! When the alarm

30

goes off, swim for your life. This last one to hit the beach will be caught by Eric Anderson.' "

Eric pummeled Steven's shoulders with the package of fish. "Now you listen. Mr. Musante said he wouldn't have come in last night either if he were a grunion."

At that, Steven and Karen laughed so hard they held their sides, and Dad told them to be quiet, and besides the hamburgers were ready.

Mom brought out a bowl of salad. She told Eric to put the fish in the refrigerator and to come right out for lunch after washing his hands.

Eric felt like a missile that had fizzled. What was wrong with his proof? Why wouldn't anyone believe it? He ate so slowly that all the hamburgers were gone and he had had only one.

That afternoon, when it was about time for Mr. Musante to take his daily run, Eric went out to the big rock and started to build a sand castle.

Soon Mr. Musante came huffing and puffing, stopping as usual to rest by the rock. But this time, Eric wasn't afraid. "Hello Mr. Musante," he said, jumping to his feet.

Mr. Musante returned the greeting. He inspected the sand castle. "Is it for a mermaid?"

Eric made sure he wasn't laughing. "Yes," he

said, dropping to the sand and molding the last turret.

"Good. I think she'll like it, especially the moat. She can swim around and around the castle."

Eric searched Mr. Musante's face. "Is the grunion make-believe, like the mermaid?"

"Not at all. Not at all."

"Why did you say if you were a grunion you wouldn't have come in last night?"

"Because I was thinking like a grunion," Mr. Musante said.

"How do you do that?"

Mr. Musante sat down on the rock. "To begin with, you must know why the grunion comes out of the ocean, onto the beach. You see, Mrs. Grunion is ready to lay her eggs. She knows that in the ocean eggs are gobbled up wholesale and she wants to lay hers where no fish will find them."

"Does she really dance on the sand?"

"What she's doing is making a nest, but it looks for all the world like she's doing one of those new-fangled dances." Mr. Musante did a couple of funny steps that made Eric laugh.

"Why didn't she come in last night when the tide was highest?" he asked.

"Because the next high tide might not be as high as this one. If she laid her eggs at the very highest tide, they might be stranded. She comes in on the second or third night of the high tides, when the waves don't come up quite as high on the beach," Mr. Musante said.

"Does it mash the eggs to walk on top of the nest?" Eric asked.

"No, because Mrs. Grunion makes her nest deep so no long-billed bird can find them. The eggs are

quite safe in their warm, damp incubator," Mr. Musante said. He pointed to the breaking waves. "Watch them. See how they break, one after another, at the same spot. After a while the tide will begin to ebb, and the water won't come up quite so high on the beach. The tide has turned. This is the exact moment when the grunion arrives. In that way she makes certain the rescuing waves two weeks later will reach the baby fish, wash them from the eggs, and whoosh them out to sea for their first swim."

Mr. Musante told Eric many other things about the little fish, and he listened carefully. "Make no mistake," Mr. Musante finished. "The grunion will be here tonight at 12:10."

After Mr. Musante left, Eric held his hands over the warm sand. He thought about the tiny fish eggs down there beneath his fingers, waiting. He had never noticed it before, but now the sand seemed alive.

A godwit came along, bobbing its head importantly at every step, probing the sand with its long bill.

"Scat," Eric said. "Scat."

The godwit began to scold, as if she had the sole right to the beach. She finally ran off, saying her name: "GodWIT! GodWIT!"

And then Eric heard Karen calling him to supper.

It was a warm evening and supper was on the patio. As soon as they started eating, Steven had an idea. "Let's go bowling tonight."

"We go bowling all the time at home," Karen said. "Let's go to a drive-in movie."

"We have one of those at home," Steven said.

Eric raised his voice. "We can't hunt grunion at home."

Steven groaned. "There's that little fish again, the one that's never there."

"It's there all right. You're the one isn't there at the right time," Eric said.

Steven rolled his eyes at Karen. "We're supposed to stand on the beach with our shovels and pails and wait for that alarm clock to ring."

"You don't use shovels. It's against the law, and it's not sporting."

"I could use my butterfly net," Karen said, giggling.

"You use your bare hands," Eric said. "Then you put the grunion in a burlap sack which you have tied around your waist. And you'd better wear a bathing suit."

"You mean we pick them right off the waves and stick them in a bag?" Steven asked.

"You don't do anything of the kind," Eric said.

"The grunion come in on one wave, lay their eggs in the sand, and you grab them with your hands after that when they're on their way back to the ocean."

Steven and Karen started laughing again, but Dad told them to be quiet. "Where did you learn all this, Eric?"

"From Mr. Musante."

"It sounds like it," Steven said. "Moustache Cup tells the kids all kinds of crazy stories about the grunion."

Eric appealed to Dad." Mr. Musante doesn't tell the kids the truth because they're greedy. They shovel up pailfuls of grunion. But they don't really want to eat the fish. For a long time there were hardly any grunion left. That's why he won't tell."

Karen sighed. "What are we going to do with Eric? He really believes that silly man."

"He isn't silly. And we've got to go tonight! They'll really be in at ten minutes after midnight."

Steven made a noise like the ringing of an alarm clock. "Hear ye, hear ye — your last chance to see the dancing fish."

Mom patted Eric's arm. "It's a little late to start fishing after midnight, don't you think?"

He'd lost. Eric looked down at his plate, trying to swallow past the hurt in his throat, blinking to keep the tears back. They wouldn't go to the beach tonight. There would be no last bonfire. He wouldn't be there when the grunion came up on the beach.

But Dad was rapping on the table. "Now everyone pipe down. Let's have a little order. I told Eric to find proof that there is a fish called grunion. He's come up with facts worth looking into. For the first time we know what we're looking for, and how to go about catching it. After supper we'll comb the beach for driftwood for our fire. Then everyone will close his eyes for a couple of hours, so we'll be bright enough to see the grunion when they show up."

Karen gasped. "You mean we really get to go down to the beach at midnight?"

"I think we can change our routine for once in the interest of natural science," Dad said.

Now everyone was excited.

"I'll make cocoa to take in the thermos," Karen said.

"I think I know where I can get some burlap sacks," Steven said.

"And I'd better check the flashlights, and see about film for the camera," Dad said.

"We'll want sandwiches," Mom said.

Eric was so filled to the brim with good feeling,

39

he couldn't talk. This was *his* family. He felt as warm and soft inside as a toasted marshmallow.

And then he had a terrible thought.

Mr. Musante had promised that the grunion would come in at 12:10.

But what if they didn't?

It was nearing midnight when the Andersons, carrying blankets, baskets and flashlights, left the

trailer. The beach was black-and-silver, empty but for two bonfires. A boy and girl playing against the brightness of the far one made fantastic silhouettes, like war-dancing Indians. As soon as Dad and Steven began to build the fire, the children came visiting.

"If you're looking for grunion, they're not running tonight," the boy said.

"It's because of the moonlight," the girl said. "They come in when it's foggy."

The more Eric listened, the more he worried. While he tied his burlap sack around his waist he thought of all the things that could happen — the grunion might come in at some other place along the beach and miss the Cove altogether. Or maybe he just wouldn't be quick enough to see them.

"It's midnight," Dad said, and Eric shivered with excitement. He ran down to the water. The waves thundered and crashed high on the beach. He stood at the limit of the waves, where they scalloped the dark sand in white, digging his toes in against the pull of water and sand. One wave come in after another; one after another. All of them reached the exact spot where he stood.

Eric waited, watching. Finally, it seemed to him that one wave fell a little short of the one before. So did the next one. And the next.

The tide had turned.

This was the moment.

Now the grunion would come in.

Where were they? Where? Where?

"Keep watching," he heard a familiar voice say. It was Mr. Musante.

Eric felt encouraged, just knowing Mr. Musante was here.

Another wave came roaring in. As the water pulled back to sea, Eric turned his back to the ocean and searched the sand.

He saw one — two — three —

"GRUNION!" he shouted. *"The grunion are running."*

Everyone came in a rush: Dad and Mom, Steven, Karen, a dog, the people from the other fires.

Another wave rolled in.

High on the sand, tearing back to the ocean, were five or six silver streaks. Eric fell to his knees. He *had* one.

Then his hands were empty. The fish had slipped away.

Eric scrambled after it. Three times he had his hands on the squirming streak before he could hold onto it.

In the moonlight he saw that it was indeed: as small as a sea horse; as shining as a star.

The wave which *his* grunion should have ridden back to sea roared out. The grunion fought to be back in the ocean, but Eric held him fast.

"Eric's got one, Eric's got one," Steven cried, just as a flash went off. That would be Dad taking a picture.

Everyone crowded around.

Eric had his grunion; his treasure.

He started to slip it into the burlap sack.

The fish was cool in his hands. Beating with life.

It made another try to get out of Eric's grasp. Was it thinking of the coral castle in the forest of reeds? Of swimming in and out of the castle's doors?

He could let it go free.

Did he really need to have his grunion in the burlap sack to prove he had a treasure.

It was so little.

And now it wasn't fighting quite so hard.

Eric dropped to his knees, opened his hands.

The grunion fairly jumped out of his fingers. It caught the next wave and rode high and gloriously out to sea.

Eric looked up. Everyone was smiling at him.

Then Mr. Musante was shouting, pointing to an incoming wave.

Tumbling along the plume of the roller were

hundreds, maybe thousands, of small fish. Like ballet dancers in silver tights, they flashed across the sand-stage, glittering, gliding, whirling. A fleeting moment, a brilliant performance, and the dancers were racing for the sea. A wave washed over them; the ballet vanished, the stage was empty.

Twice the pantomime was repeated, before the final curtain.

And only then did the watchers move or talk.

"Fantastic," Steven said.

"Did it really happen?" Karen asked.

"I wouldn't believe it if I hadn't seen it," Mom said.

"We'll never forget it, any of us," Dad said.

Everyone was thanking Mr. Musante for telling Eric about the grunion, and Mom was inviting him for hot chocolate, and Dad was leading the way up the beach to the fire.

But Eric held back for one last look at the sea where his grunion lived. He would always remember how it felt to hold the little fish: like trying to stop a waterfall, or grasp a shooting star.

Eric thought maybe his grunion was the only one to have escaped captivity; the only one to have missed the first wave home, and then to have caught the second.

The Author

DALE FIFE has written two previous books for young readers, *A Stork for the Bell Tower* and *Who's in Charge of Lincoln?* Mrs. Fife lives in San Mateo, California.

One of Mrs. Fife's main interests is the region of Alsace in Europe, the setting of *A Stork for the Bell Tower*. Mrs. Fife's mother was born there and Dale Fife has visited the village where her mother grew up. One of Mrs. Fife's hobbies is collecting recipes of Old Alsace, which usually begin "take six eggs, a cup of cream," etc., etc.

The Artist

MARILYN MILLER was born in San Francisco, California. She attended the California School of Fine Arts and specialized in lithography. Then she moved to New York City with a scholarship to the Art Students League.

In addition to her work as an illustrator of children's books, Marilyn Miller has done magazine and newspaper illustration. Her work has appeared in one-man shows and is represented in private, college and library collections.

Marilyn Miller and her husband who is also an artist live in Connecticut with their two children.